Defoe
Abbott
Marx
Hardy
Machiavelli
Montaigne
Chesterton
Cooper
Emerson
Haggard
Joyce
Austen
Hugo
Eliot
Grimm
Melville
Stoker
Carroll
Christie
Maupassant
Molière
Byron
Schiller
Wilde
Garnett
Einstein
Fitzgerald
Engels
Smith
Kafka
Goethe
Hawthorne
Hall
Cotton
Dostoyevsky
Willis
Baum
Henry
Kipling
Doyle
Leslie
Dumas
Flaubert
Nietzsche
Stockton
Turgenev
Balzac
Burroughs
Vatsyayana
Crane
Verne
Curtis
Tocqueville
Whitman
Gogol
Vinci
Homer
Widger
Tolstoy
Busch
Darwin
Thoreau
Twain
Potter
Freud
Zola
Lawrence
Scott
Plato
Harte
Kant
Jowett
Stevenson
Dickens
Andersen
Burton
London
Descartes
Cervantes
Hesse
Poe
Aristotle
Wells
Voltaire
Hale
James
Hastings
Cooke
Bunner
Shakespeare
Richter
Chambers
Irving
da
Dante
Chekhov
Shaw
Benedict
Alcott
Doré
Swift
Wodehouse
Pushkin
Newton

 tredition®

tredition was established in 2006 by Sandra Latusseck and Soenke Schulz. Based in Hamburg, Germany, tredition offers publishing solutions to authors and publishing houses, combined with world-wide distribution of printed and digital book content. tredition is uniquely positioned to enable authors and publishing houses to create books on their own terms and without conventional manufacturing risks.

For more information please visit: www.tredition.com

TREDITION CLASSICS

This book is part of the TREDITION CLASSICS series. The creators of this series are united by passion for literature and driven by the intention of making all public domain books available in printed format again - worldwide. Most TREDITION CLASSICS titles have been out of print and off the bookstore shelves for decades. At tredition we believe that a great book never goes out of style and that its value is eternal. Several mostly non-profit literature projects provide content to tredition. To support their good work, tredition donates a portion of the proceeds from each sold copy. As a reader of a TREDITION CLASSICS book, you support our mission to save many of the amazing works of world literature from oblivion. See all available books at www.tredition.com.

Project Gutenberg

The content for this book has been graciously provided by Project Gutenberg. Project Gutenberg is a non-profit organization founded by Michael Hart in 1971 at the University of Illinois. The mission of Project Gutenberg is simple: To encourage the creation and distribution of eBooks. Project Gutenberg is the first and largest collection of public domain eBooks.

Bib Ballads

Ring Lardner

Imprint

This book is part of TREDITION CLASSICS

Author: Ring Lardner
Cover design: Buchgut, Berlin – Germany

Publisher: tredition GmbH, Hamburg - Germany
ISBN: 978-3-8472-1282-9

www.tredition.com
www.tredition.de

BIB BALLADS

BY
RING W. LARDNER

ILLUSTRATED BY
FONTAINE FOX

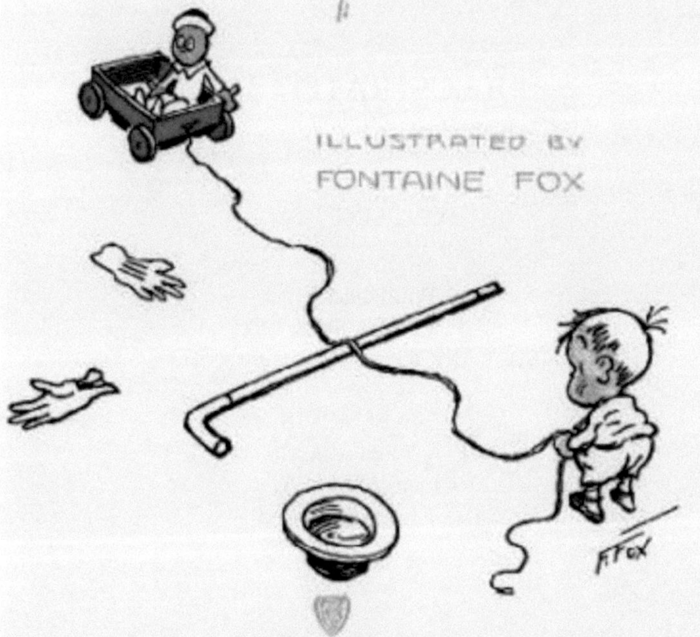

Published by
P. F. VOLLAND & CO.
NEW YORK   CHICAGO   TORONTO

BIB BALLADS

BY

RING W. LARDNER

ILLUSTRATED BY

FONTAINE FOX

Published by
P. F. VOLLAND & CO.
NEW YORK CHICAGO TORONTO

CONTENTS

FOREWORD

Dear Parents: — Don't imagine, please,
It's in a boastful spirit
I fashion verses such as these;
That's not the truth or near it.

A hundred or a thousand, yes,
A million kids there may be
Who aren't one iota less
Attractive than this baby.

I'll venture that your household has
As valuable a treasure
As mine, but mine I know, and as
For yours, I've not that pleasure.

And that is why my book's about
Just one, O Dads and Mothers;
But babes are babes, and mine, no doubt,
Is very much like others.

THE AUTHOR

BIB BALLADS

GOOD-BY BILL

Dollar Bill, that I've held so tight
Ever since payday, a week ago,
Shall I purchase with you tonight
A pair of seats at the vaudeville show?
(Hark! A voice from the easy chair:
"Look at his shoes! We must buy a pair.")

Dollar Bill, from the wreckage saved,
Tell me, how shall I squander you?
Shall I be shined, shampooed and shaved,
Singed and trimmed 'round the edges, too?
(Hark! A voice from the easy chair:
"He hasn't a romper that's fit to wear.")

Dollar Bill, that I cherished so,
Think of the cigarettes you'd buy,
Turkish ones, with a kick, you know;
Makin's eventually tire a guy.
(Hark! A voice from the easy chair:
"Look at those stockings! Just one big tear!")

Dollar Bill, it is time to part.
What do I care for a vaudeville show?
I'll shave myself and look just as smart.
Makin's aren't so bad, you know.
Dollar Bill, we must say good-by;
There on the floor is the Reason Why.

A VISIT FROM YOUNG GLOOM

There's been a young stranger at our house,
A baby whom nobody knew;
Who hated his brother, his father, his mother,
And made them aware of it, too.

He stayed with us nearly a fortnight
And carried a grouch all the while,
Nor promise nor present could make him look pleasant;
He hadn't the power to smile.

He cried when he couldn't have something;
He cried just as hard when he could;
Kind words by the earful but made him more tearful,
And scoldings did just as much good.

He stormed when his meals weren't ready,
And when they *were* ready, he screamed.
He went to bed growling, got up again howling
And quarreled and snarled as he dreamed.

He's gone, and the child we are fond of
Is back, just as nice as of old.
But I hope to be in some port European
The next time he has a bad cold.

AN APPRECIATIVE AUDIENCE

My son, I wish that it were half
As easy to extract a laugh
From grown-ups as from thee.
Then I'd go on the stage, my boy,
While Richard Carle and Eddie Foy
Burned up with jealousy.

I wouldn't have to rack my brain
Or lie awake all night in vain
Pursuit of brand new jokes;
Nor fear my lines were heard with groans
Of pain and sympathetic moans
From sympathetic folks.

I'd merely have to make a face,
Just twist a feature out of place,
And be the soul of wit;
Or bark, and then pretend to bite,
And, from the screams of wild delight,
Be sure I'd made a hit.

DISCIPLINE

He couldn't have a doughnut, and it made him very mad;
He undertook to get revenge by screaming at his dad.

"Cut out that noise!" I ordered, and he gave another roar,
And so I put him in "the room" and shut and locked the door.

I left him in his prison cell two minutes, just about,
And, penitent, he smiled at me when I did let him out.

But when he got another look at the forbidden fruit
He gave a yell that they could hear in Jacksonville or Butte.

"Cut out that noise!" I barked again. "Cut out that foghorn stuff!
Perhaps I didn't leave you in your prison long enough.

"You want your dad to keep you jailed all afternoon, I guess."
He smiled at me and answered his equivalent for "yes."

INEXPENSIVE GUESTS

I wonder how 'twould make you feel,
My fellow food providers,
To have as guests at ev'ry meal
Three—count 'em, three—outsiders.

Well, that's the case with me, but still
I don't complain or holler,
For, strange to say, the groc'ry bill
Has not gone up a dollar.

These guests of ours, to make it brief,
Can't really chew or swallow;
They're merely dolls, called Indian Chief,
And Funny Man, and Rollo.

HIS SENSE OF HUMOR

Perhaps in some respects it's true
That you resemble dad;
To be informed I look like you
Would never make me mad.
But one thing I am sure of, son,
You have a different line
Of humor, your idea of fun
Is not a bit like mine.

You drop my slippers in the sink
And leave them there to soak.
That's very laughable, you think
But I can't see the joke
You take my hat outdoors with you
And fill it full of earth;
You seem to think that's witty, too,
But I'm not moved to mirth.

You open up the chicken-yard;
Its inmates run a mile;
You giggle, but I find it hard
To force one-half a smile.
No, kid, I fear your funny stuff,
Though funny it may be,
Is not quite delicate enough
To make a hit with me.

SPEECH ECONOMY

Since he began to talk and sing,
I've learned one interesting thing—
The value of a verb is small;
In fact, it has no worth at all.

Why waste the breath required to say,
"While toddling through the park today,
I saw a bird up in a tree,"
When "Twee, pahk, birt," does splendidly?

Why should one say, "Please pass the bread,"
When "Ba-ba me" is easier said?

And why "I'm starved. Have supper quick,"
When "LUNCH!" yelled loudly, does the trick?

Why "I've been riding on a train,"
When "By-by, Choo-choo" makes it plain?
"Let words be few," the poet saith,
So leave out words and save your breath.

WELCOME TO SPRING

Spring, you are welcome, for you are the friend of
Fathers of all little girlies and chaps.
Spring, you are welcome, for you mean the end of
Bundling them up in their cold-weather wraps.

Breathes there a parent of masculine gender,
One whose young hopeful is seven or less,
Who never has cursed the designer and vender
Of juvenile-out-of-doors-winter-time dress?

Leggings and overcoat, rubbers that squeeze on,
Mittens and sweater a trifle too small;
Not in the lot is one thing you can ease on,
One that's affixed with no trouble at all.

Spring, you are welcome, thrice welcome to father;
Not for your flowers and birds, I'm afraid,
As much as your promised relief from the bother
Of bundling the kid for the daily parade.

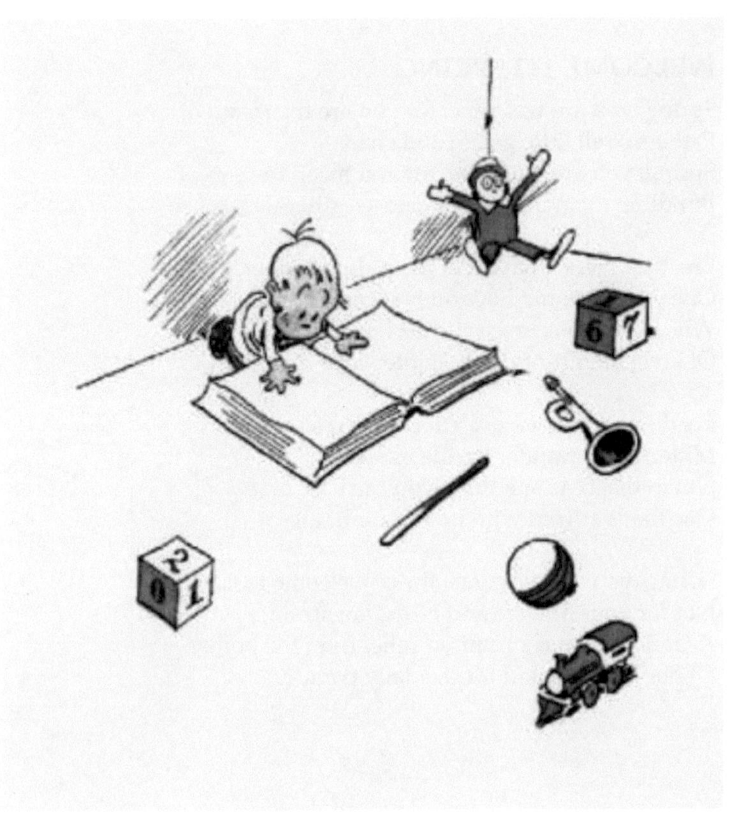

TASTE

I can't understand why you pass up the toys
That Santa considered just right for small boys;
I can't understand why you turn up your nose
At dogs, hobby-horses, and treasures like those,
And play a whole hour, sometimes longer than that,
With a thing as prosaic as daddy's old hat.

The tables and shelves have been loaded for you
With volumes of pictures—they're pretty ones, too—
Of birds, beasts, and fishes, and old Mother Goose

Repines in a corner and feels like the deuce,
While you, on the floor, quite contentedly look
At page after page of the telephone book.

RIDDLES

If it's fun to take books from the bookcase,
If you really believe it's worth while
To carry them out to the kitchen
And build them all up in a pile,
Why isn't it just as agreeable then
To carry them back to the bookcase again?

If it's fun to make marks with a pencil

In books that one cares for a heap;
To tear out the pages from volumes
One likes and is anxious to keep,
Why isn't it pleasure to put on the hummer
A magazine read and discarded last summer?

HESITATION

I've orders to waken you from your nap,
And orders are orders, my little chap.
But I hate to do it, because it seems
A shame to break in on your blissful dreams.

I've sat and watched you a long, long while,
And not since I came have you ceased to smile.
So it strikes me as wrong to arouse you, boy,
From sleep that's so plainly a sleep of joy.

'Twill make a big diff'rence tonight, of course,
But p'rhaps you are riding a real live horse;
In dreams, it's a pleasant and harmless sport,
So why should I cruelly cut it short?

Maybe you have for your very own
A piece of pie or an ice cream cone;
If that's your amusement, why end it quick?
Dream-food can't possibly make you sick.

Orders are orders and I'm afraid
It's trouble for me if they're disobeyed.
But I'll bet if the boss could see you, son,
She'd put off the duty, as I have done.

HIS WONDERFUL CHOO-CHOOS

When I see his wonderful choo-choo trains,
Which he daily builds with infinite pains,
Whose cars are a crazy and curious lot—
A doll, a picture, a pepper pot,
A hat, a pillow, a horse, a book,
A pote, a mintie, a button hook,
A bag of tobacco, a piece of string,
A pair of wubbas, a bodkin ring,
A deck of twos and a paper box,
A brush, a comb and a lot of blocks—
When I first gaze on his wonderful trains,
Which he daily builds with infinite pains,
I laugh, and I think to myself, "O gee!
Was ever a child as cute as he?"

But when he's gone to his cozy nest,
From the toil of his strenuous day to rest,
And when I gaze on his trains once more,
Where they lie, abandoned, across the floor,
And when the terrible task I face
Of putting each "Pullman" back in its place,
I groan a little, and think, "O gee!
Was ever a child as mean as he?"

GLOSSARY
Bodkin—A napkin
Mintie—A mitten.
Pote—A pencil.
Twos—Cards.

COUSINLY AFFECTION

Why do you love your Cousin Paull?
For his sweet face, his smile, and all
The little tricks that charm us so?
You're not quite old enough to know
How cute he is; to realize
How clever for a child his size.
I'm sure you can't appreciate
The things that make us think him great.

And yet you love your Cousin Paull.
Is it because he's twice as small
As you, just right for you to maul?
Because he won't fight back, or bawl?
Because when he is pushed he'll fall?
And, where most kids would howl and squall,
He takes it, nor puts in a call
For mother? Am I warm at all?
Is this why you love Cousin Paull?

MY BABY'S GARDEN

My baby has a garden,
"Planted" four days ago,
And nearly half his waking hours
He spends among his precious flowers
With sprinkling can and hoe.

My baby has a garden,
And Oh, how proud he is
When, yielding to his pleading, we
Lay work aside and go to see
This masterpiece of his!

Behold my baby's garden,
Close by a rubbish pile!
Look at the sprinkling can and hoe
And flowers; then tell me if you know
Whether to sigh or smile.

The flowers in baby's garden,
Flat on the ground they lie,
Two hyacinths, a withered pair,
Plucked from the pile of rubbish, where
They had been left to die.

The flowers in baby's garden,
"Planted" four days ago,
Grow every hour a sadder sight,
Weaker and sicklier, in spite
Of sprinkling can and hoe.

DECISION REVERSED

32

When I mixed with the shoppers and fought in vain
To get what I sought, in the Christmas rush;
When they stood on my toes in the crowded train,
Or dented my ribs in the sidewalk crush,
I dropped my manners and snarled and swore,
And thought: "It's a bothersome, beastly bore!"

But when, at the Christmas dawn, they brought
My kid to the room where his things were piled,
And when, from my vantage point, I caught
The look on his face, I murmured: "Child,
Your dad was a fool when he snarled and swore,
And called it a bothersome, beastly bore."

THE GROCERY MAN AND THE BEAR

He was weary of all of his usual joys;
His books and his blocks made him tired,
And so did his games and mechanical toys,
And the songs he had always admired;
So I told him a story, a story so new

It had never been heard anywhere;
A tale disconnected, unlikely, untrue,
Called The Grocery Man and the Bear.

I didn't think much of the story despite
The fact 'twas a child of my brain.
And I never dreamt, when I told it that night,
That I'd have to tell it again;
I never imagined 'twould make such a hit
With the audience of one that was there
That for hours at a time he would quietly sit
Through The Grocery Man and the Bear.

To all other stories, this one is preferred;
It's the season's best seller by far,
And out at our house it's as frequently heard
As cuss-words in Mexico are.
When choo-choos and horses and picture books fail,
He'll remain, quite content, in his chair,
While I tell o'er and o'er the incredible tale
Of The Grocery Man and the Bear.

COMING HOME

Prepare for noise, you quiet walls!
You floors, get set for heavy falls!
Frail dishes, hide away!
Get ready for some scratches, stairs!
Clean table linen, say your prayers!
The kid comes home today!

For three long weeks you've been, O House,
As noiseless as the well-known mouse,
As silent as the tomb.
And you've stayed neat, with none on hand

To track your floors with mud and sand,
To muss your ev'ry room.

The ideal place for work you've been,
But soon a Bedlam once again,
A mess, a wreck. But say,
I wonder will it make us mad.
No, House, I'll bet we both are glad
The kid comes home today.

HIS IMAGINATION

One thing that's yours, my little child
Your poor old dad is simply wild
To own. It's not a book or toy;
It's your imagination, boy.
If I possessed it, what a time
I'd have, nor need to spend a dime!

I wish that I could get astride
A broom, and have a horse to ride;
Or climb into the swing, and be
A sailor on the deep blue sea,
Or b'lieve a chair a choo-choo train,
Bound anywhere and back again.

If I could ride as fast and far
On ship or horse, in train or car,
As you, at small expense or none,
If I could have one-half your fun
And do the things that you do, free,
I'd give them back my salary.

HIS MEMORY

Besides my little son's imagination,
Another thing he has appeals to me
And agitates my envious admiration—
It's his accommodating memory.

An instant after some unlucky stumble
Has floored him and induced a howl of pain,
He's clean forgotten all about his tumble
And violently sets out to romp again.

But if, when I leave home, I say that maybe
I'll get him something nice while I'm away,
It's very safe to bet that Mr. Baby
Will not forget, though I be gone all day.

Ah, would I might lose sight of things unpleasant:
The bills I owe; the work I haven't done.
And only think of future joys and present,
Like the approaching payday, and my son.

CONFESSION

A sleuth like Pinkerton or Burns
Is told that there has been a crime.
He runs down clues and leads, and learns
Who did the deed, in course of time.
It's just the other way with me:
The first thing I am sure of is
The criminal's identity,
And then I learn what crime was his.

When Son comes up with hanging head
And smiles a certain kind of smile,
When he's affectionate instead
Of playful; when he stalls awhile
And starts to speak and stops again,
Or, squirming like a mouse that's caught,
Asserts, "I am a GOOD boy," then
I look to see what harm's been wrought.

HIS LADY FRIEND

Who is Sylvia? What is she
That early every morning
You desert your family
And rush to see her, scorning
Your once cherished ma and me?

Are her playthings such a treat?
I will steal 'em from her;
Better that than not to meet
My son and heir all summer,
Save when he comes home to eat.

Or is she herself the one
And only real attraction?
Has your little heart begun
To get that sort of action?
Better wait a few years, son.

DECLARATION OF INDEPENDENCE

"MYSELF!" It means that you don't care
To have me lift you in your chair;
That if I do, you'll rage and tear.

"MYSELF!" It means you don't require

Assistance from your willing sire
In eating; 'twill but rouse your ire.

"MYSELF!" It means when you are through
That you don't want your daddy to
Unseat you, as he used to do.

Time was, and not so long ago,
When you were carried to and fro
And waited on, but now? No! No!

You'd rather fall and break your head,
Or fill your lap with cream and bread
Than be helped up or down, or fed.

Well, kid, I hope you'll stay that way
And that there'll never come a day
When you're without the strength to say,
"MYSELF!"

THE ETERNAL GREETING

What is the welcoming word I hear
When I reach home at the close of day?
"Glad you are with us, daddy, dear?"
Something I'd like to hear you say?
No, it is this, invariably:
"Daddy, what have you got for me?"

"Deep affection," I might reply;
What would it profit if I did?
I might answer: "The price to buy

Clothes and edibles for you, kid."
You would repeat, insistently:
"Daddy, what have you got for me?"

Isn't my Self enough for you?
Doesn't my Presence satisfy?
No, that spelling would never do;
You want Presents, a new supply,
When you inquire so eagerly:
"Daddy, what have you got for me?"

'Twould be much nicer and cheaper, son,
If I were welcome without a toy,
But as I'm not, I must purchase one
And take my reward from your look of joy
When you open the bundle and cry: "O, see!
See what daddy has got for me!"

GUESS AGAIN

"I guess I'll help you, daddy."
And daddy can't say "No;"
For if he did, 'twould wound you, kid,
And cause the tears to flow.

"I guess I'll help you, daddy."
And daddy says: "All right,"
And tries to do, ignoring you,
Whatever work's in sight.

But what's the use of trying?
As well be reconciled
To quit and play the game that may
Be pleasing to you, child.

To quit and play, or roughhouse,
Or read, as you elect;
For I'm afraid the guess you made
Was wholly incorrect.

NEARLY A SINECURE

"I'm going to the office."
So says my youngster, and
Gets on the train to take him there
(The train's the sofa or a chair,
Whichever's near at hand.)

"Now I am to the office.
I'm working now," says he,

And just continues standing there
On that same lounge or that same chair,
As idle as can be.

Perhaps four seconds after
He first got on his train,
I see him getting off once more.
He steps or falls onto the floor
And says, "I'm home again."

I don't know what they pay him,
Nor where the office is.
The nature of the boy's posish
I've never learned — but how I wish
I had that job of his!

THE HECKUSES

That may not be the proper way
To spell their name; I cannot say.
I've never seen 'em written out:
I've only heard 'em talked about.
They're coming here tonight to dine,
So says that little son of mine.
But all last week, 'twas just the same;

They were to come, and never came.

And I'm just skeptical enough
To think they're all a myth, a bluff;
Mere creatures of my youngster's brain,
Whose coming he'll await in vain.
And yet to him they're very real.
They own a big black auto'bile.
They work downtown, and they'll arrive
Out here at one-two-three-four-five.

The Heckuses are four all told.
There's Mrs. H. who's very old,
And Baby Heckus, and a lad
Named Tom, and Bill, the Heckus dad.
Beyond this point I can't describe
The fascinating Heckus tribe.
I can but wonder how he came
To think of such a lovely name.

HIS FAVORITE ROLE

You could be president as well as not,
Since all you'd have to do is think you were,
With that imagination that you've got;
Or multimillionaire if you prefer,
Or you could be some famous football star,
Or Tyrus Cobb, admired by ev'ry fan;
Instead of that, you tell me that you are
The Garbage Man.

Why pick him out, when you can take your choice?
Is his so charming, nice, and sweet a role
That acting it should make you to rejoice
And be a source of comfort to your soul?
Is there some hidden happiness that he
Uncovers in his march from can to can
That you above all else should want to be
The Garbage Man?

THE PATHS OF RASHNESS

Up to the sky the birdman flew
And looped some loops that were bold and new.
The people marvelled at nerve so great
And gasped or cheered as he tempted fate,
More daring each day than the day before,
Till the birdman fell and arose no more.

The bandit bragged of his daylight crimes

And said: "I'm the wonder of modern times."
Bolder and bolder his thefts became,
And the people shook when they heard his name.
He boasted: "I'm one that they'll never get."
But he jollied himself into Joliet.

Well, son, I suppose you would be admired
For the valorous habit that you've acquired
Of rushing at each little girl you meet
And hugging her tight in the public street.
But the day will come, I have not a doubt,
When you'll stagger home with an eye scratched out.

THE NEW PLAYTHING

I wonder what your thought will be
And what you'll say and do, sir,
When you come home again and see
What Daddy's got for you, sir.

I wonder if you'll like it, boy,
Or turn away disgusted
(You've often scorned a nice, new toy

For one that's old and busted.)

I wonder if you'll laugh, or cry
And run in fright to mother,
Or just act bored to death, when I
Show you your brand new brother.